Where Do The Christmas Trees Go?

Written and Illustrated by Joanne Ferrante

Window Seat Publishing, Inc.
West Hempstead, NY

This book is dedicated
to my father and mother for all the
wonderful Christmas morning memories
they gave to us.

It was a week and a half since Christmas. Matty was sitting by the big window in his living room. He was staring out at the curb where his Christmas tree was lying. Suddenly John, Matty's big brother, plopped down on the couch beside him.

"It looks like it's sleeping," said Matty.

"What does?" asked John.

"Our Christmas tree." said Matty.

"Oh," said John. He quickly glanced out the window to look at their tree.

"Where do you think they go John?" asked Matty.

"In the garbage," said John yawning.

J. Leopold Ferrante

"After that," said Matty. "After the garbage truck takes them away, where do they go?"

"They go to the garbage dump," said John. "Where else?"

"But after that," said Matty. "After they get to the dump where do they go?"

"I don't know," said John getting annoyed. Maybe they go to a Christmas tree heaven or something. Who knows?"

"But I want to know," cried Matty. "They have to go somewhere! They just have to! I love our Christmas tree. He was the best tree we ever had. He just can't go in the garbage!" Now Matty was getting annoyed too.

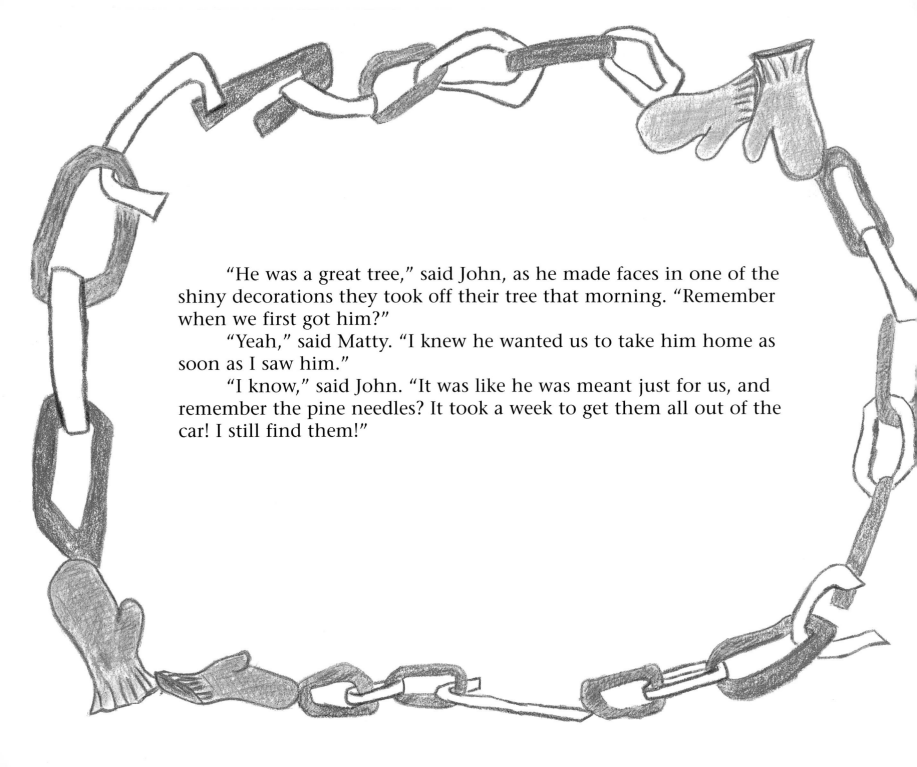

"He was a great tree," said John, as he made faces in one of the shiny decorations they took off their tree that morning. "Remember when we first got him?"

"Yeah," said Matty. "I knew he wanted us to take him home as soon as I saw him."

"I know," said John. "It was like he was meant just for us, and remember the pine needles? It took a week to get them all out of the car! I still find them!"

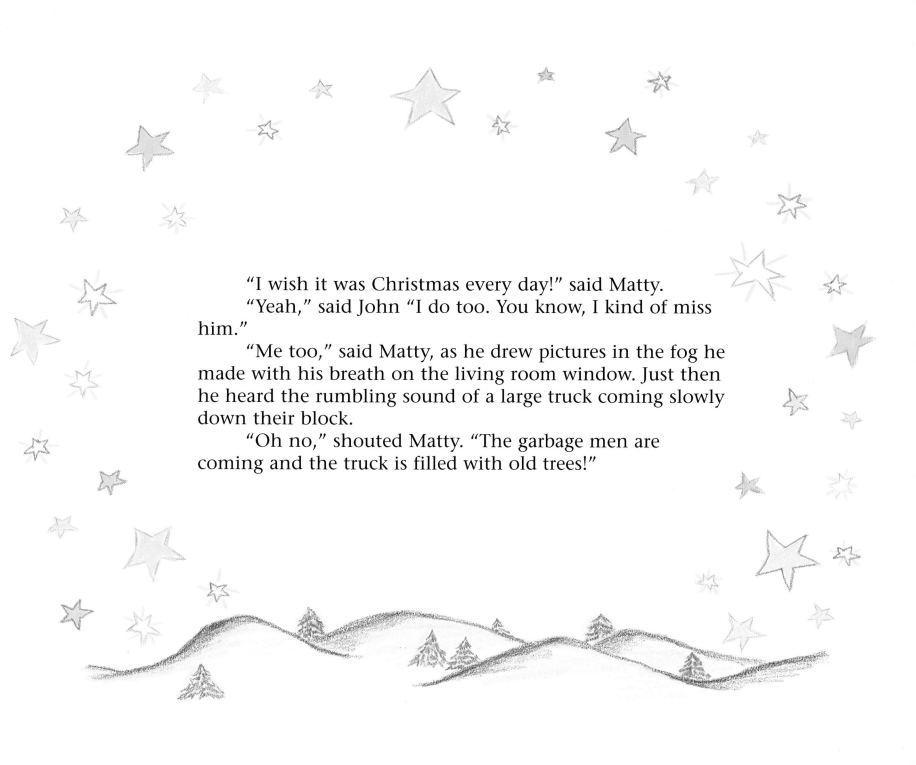

"I wish it was Christmas every day!" said Matty.

"Yeah," said John "I do too. You know, I kind of miss him."

"Me too," said Matty, as he drew pictures in the fog he made with his breath on the living room window. Just then he heard the rumbling sound of a large truck coming slowly down their block.

"Oh no," shouted Matty. "The garbage men are coming and the truck is filled with old trees!"

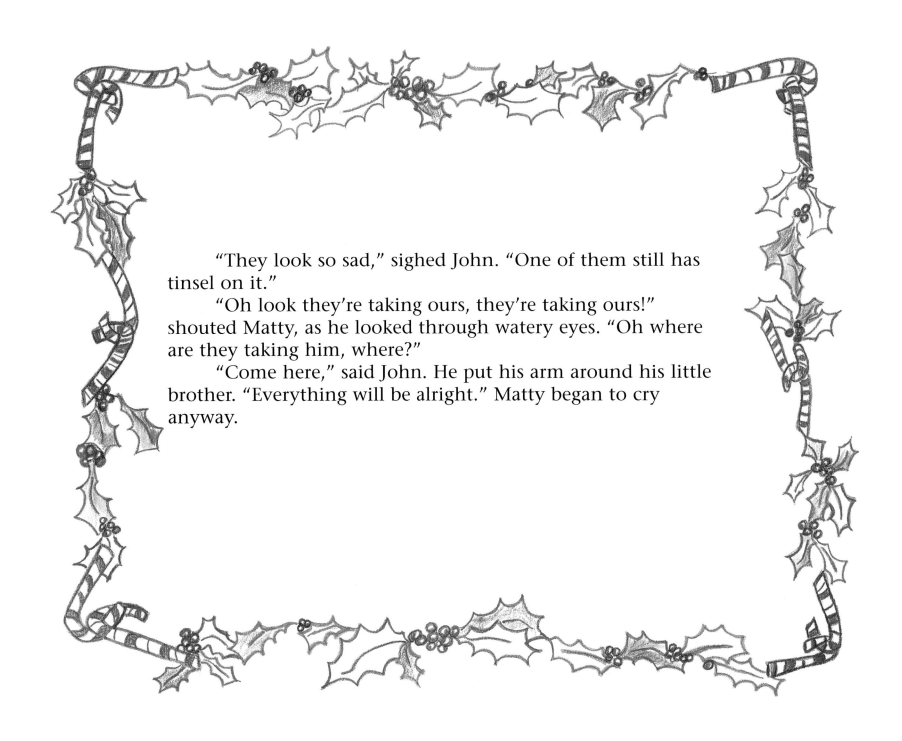

"They look so sad," sighed John. "One of them still has tinsel on it."

"Oh look they're taking ours, they're taking ours!" shouted Matty, as he looked through watery eyes. "Oh where are they taking him, where?"

"Come here," said John. He put his arm around his little brother. "Everything will be alright." Matty began to cry anyway.

"I just want to know if our tree is all right. Maybe he's cold or needs water or something," cried Matty with a sniffle. John also began to feel very sad about their old buddy.

"Now I'm beginning to wonder where they go," he said softly.

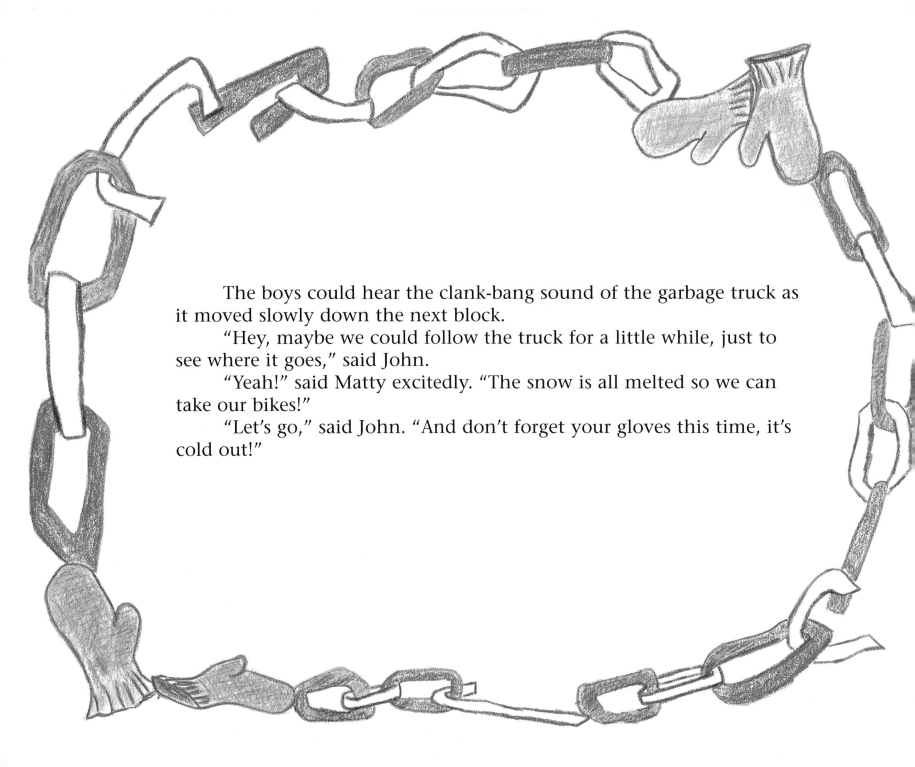

The boys could hear the clank-bang sound of the garbage truck as it moved slowly down the next block.

"Hey, maybe we could follow the truck for a little while, just to see where it goes," said John.

"Yeah!" said Matty excitedly. "The snow is all melted so we can take our bikes!"

"Let's go," said John. "And don't forget your gloves this time, it's cold out!"

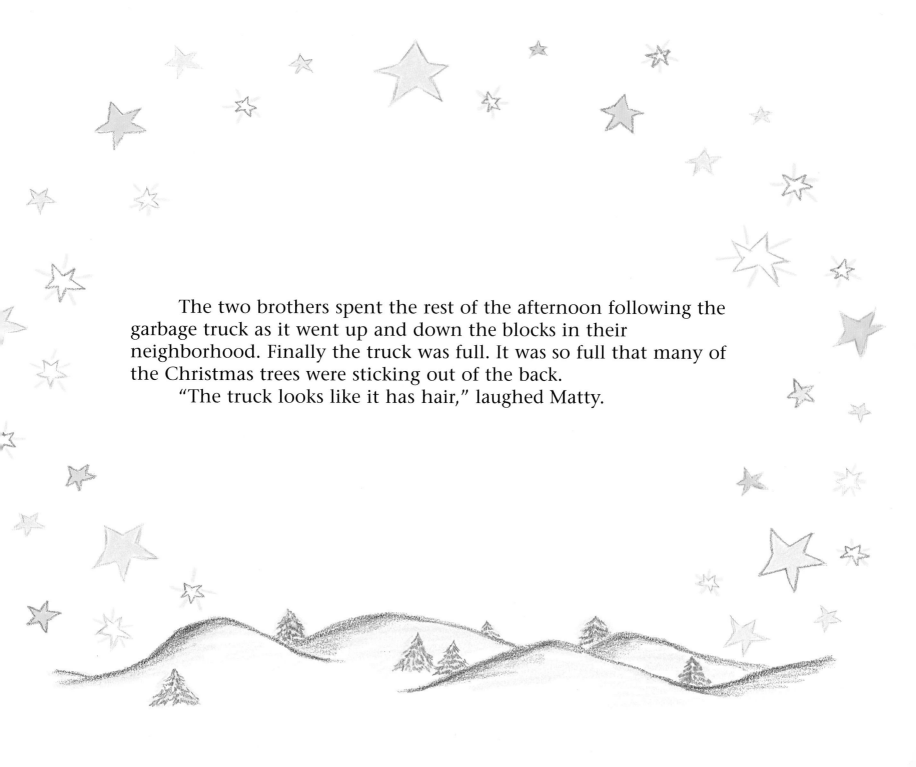

The two brothers spent the rest of the afternoon following the garbage truck as it went up and down the blocks in their neighborhood. Finally the truck was full. It was so full that many of the Christmas trees were sticking out of the back.

"The truck looks like it has hair," laughed Matty.

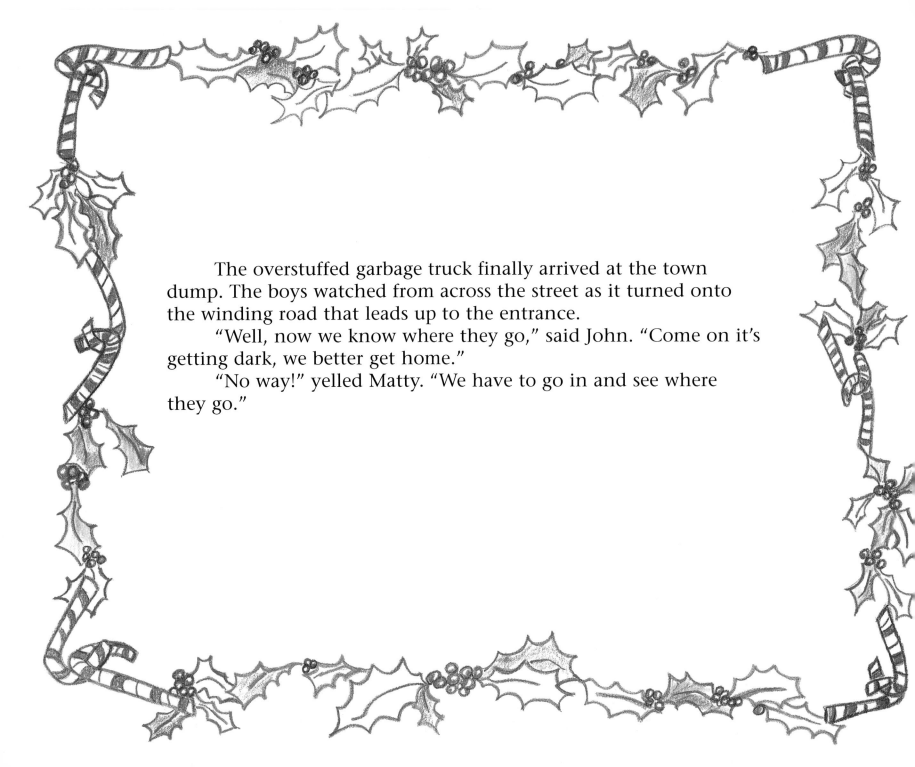

The overstuffed garbage truck finally arrived at the town dump. The boys watched from across the street as it turned onto the winding road that leads up to the entrance.

"Well, now we know where they go," said John. "Come on it's getting dark, we better get home."

"No way!" yelled Matty. "We have to go in and see where they go."

"Matty," pleaded John. "Come on it's getting late and besides it smells really bad!"

"No, I'm not leaving!" shouted Matty and he started to ride into the dump.

"Okay, okay," said John. "But just for a little while. Look it's dark now." The boys started walking their bikes up the long winding road. They looked all around with wide eyes as the moonlight seemed to add a sparkle and shine to the mountains and mountains of garbage.

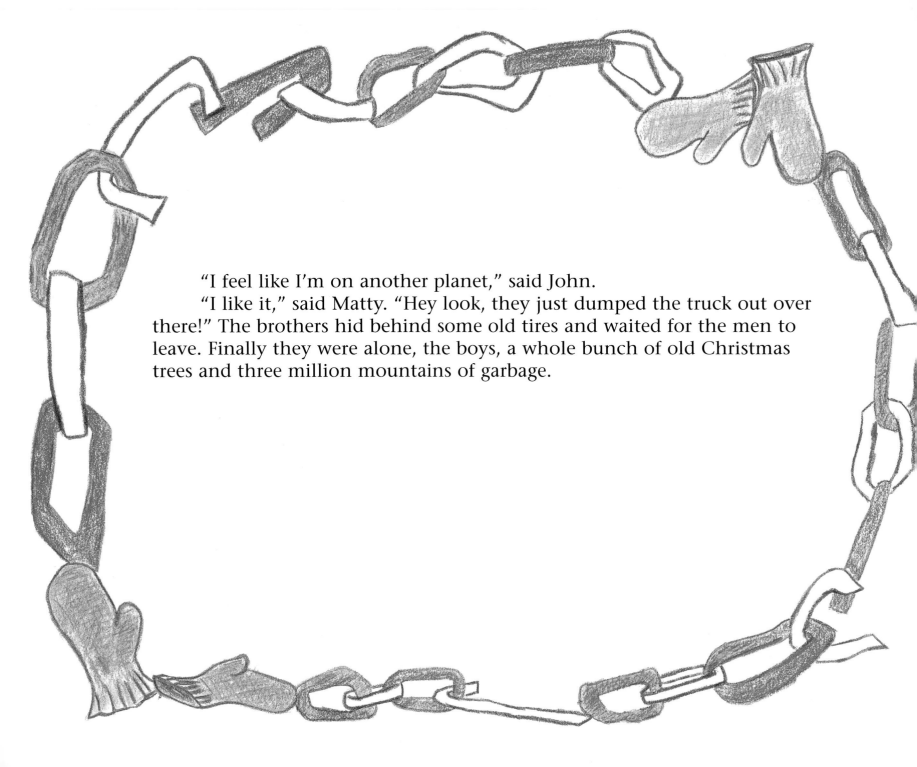

"I feel like I'm on another planet," said John.

"I like it," said Matty. "Hey look, they just dumped the truck out over there!" The brothers hid behind some old tires and waited for the men to leave. Finally they were alone, the boys, a whole bunch of old Christmas trees and three million mountains of garbage.

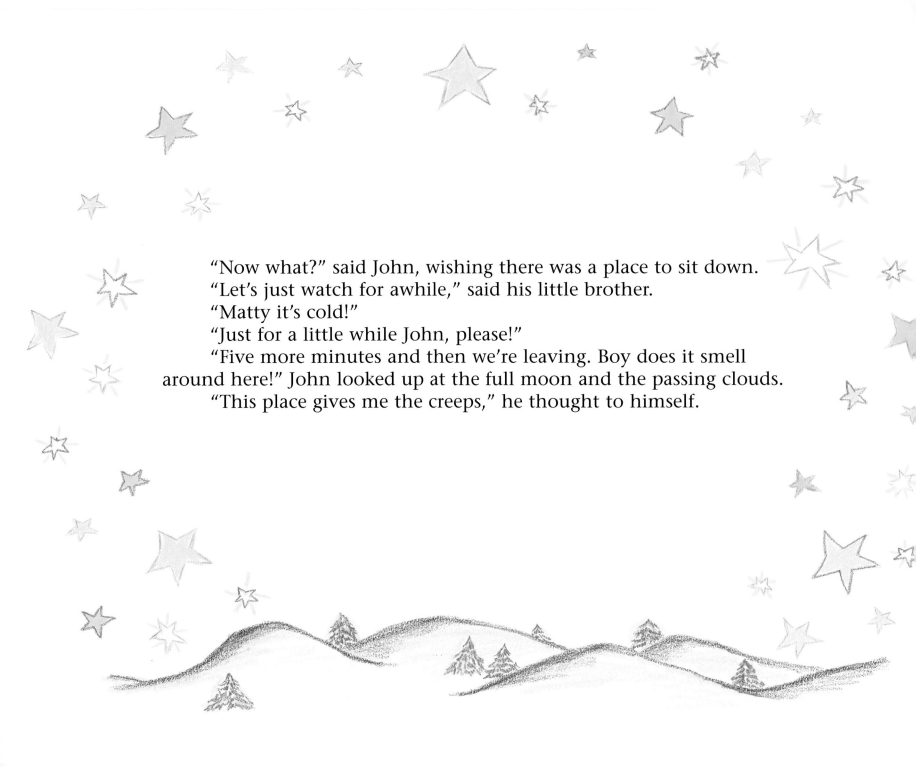

"Now what?" said John, wishing there was a place to sit down.
"Let's just watch for awhile," said his little brother.
"Matty it's cold!"
"Just for a little while John, please!"
"Five more minutes and then we're leaving. Boy does it smell around here!" John looked up at the full moon and the passing clouds.
"This place gives me the creeps," he thought to himself.

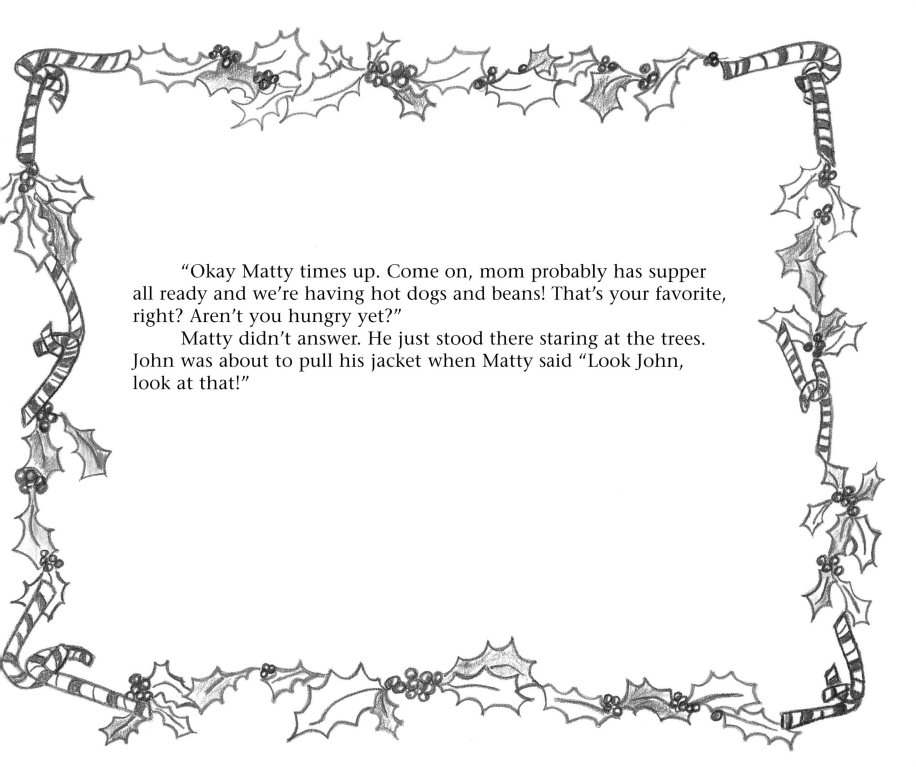

"Okay Matty times up. Come on, mom probably has supper all ready and we're having hot dogs and beans! That's your favorite, right? Aren't you hungry yet?"

Matty didn't answer. He just stood there staring at the trees. John was about to pull his jacket when Matty said "Look John, look at that!"

"At what?" asked John.

"Look at that little fire! That wasn't there before!"

"Oh there's probably a million little fires around here," explained John.

"Well that's the only one that I see and it wasn't there before!" said Matty getting angry.

"Shhh," said John. "I think it's getting bigger!"

"It is!" whispered Matty excitedly.

"Did you see that?" whispered John.
"See what?" said Matty with big eyes.
"That tree, I think it moved!"
"Stop trying to scare me John.... oh.... it did move!"
"Shhh, whisper!" said John as he pulled his brother down beside him.
"Look there's another one!" said Matty grabbing Johns arm.
"Let go, you're going to knock me over!"
"I think they're all moving.... Look John look!"
"What the heck is going on?" whispered John.

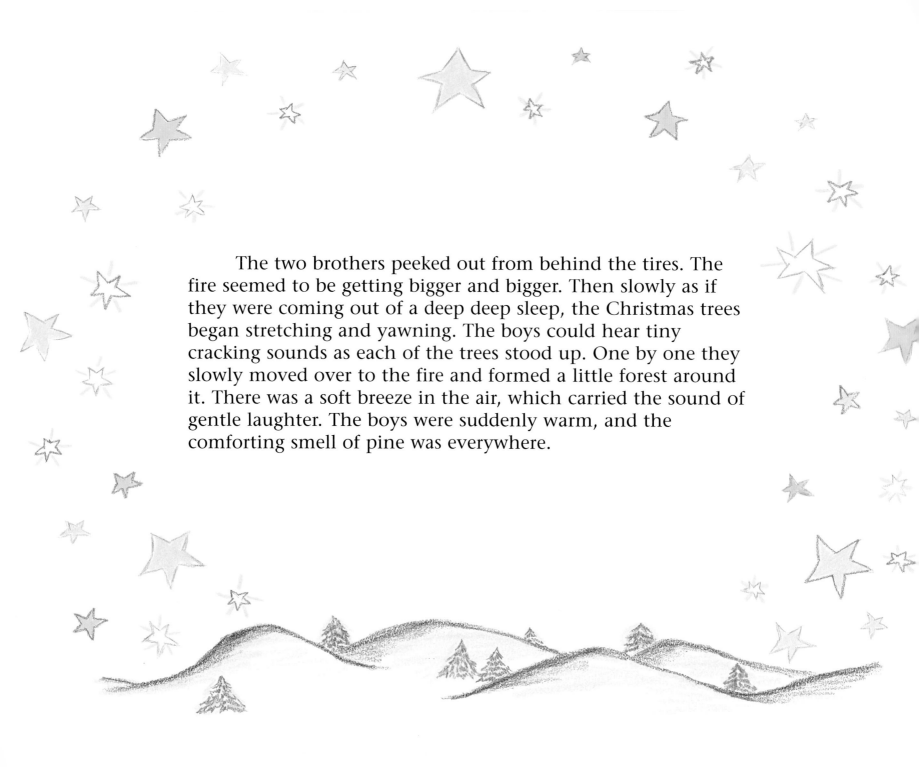

The two brothers peeked out from behind the tires. The fire seemed to be getting bigger and bigger. Then slowly as if they were coming out of a deep deep sleep, the Christmas trees began stretching and yawning. The boys could hear tiny cracking sounds as each of the trees stood up. One by one they slowly moved over to the fire and formed a little forest around it. There was a soft breeze in the air, which carried the sound of gentle laughter. The boys were suddenly warm, and the comforting smell of pine was everywhere.

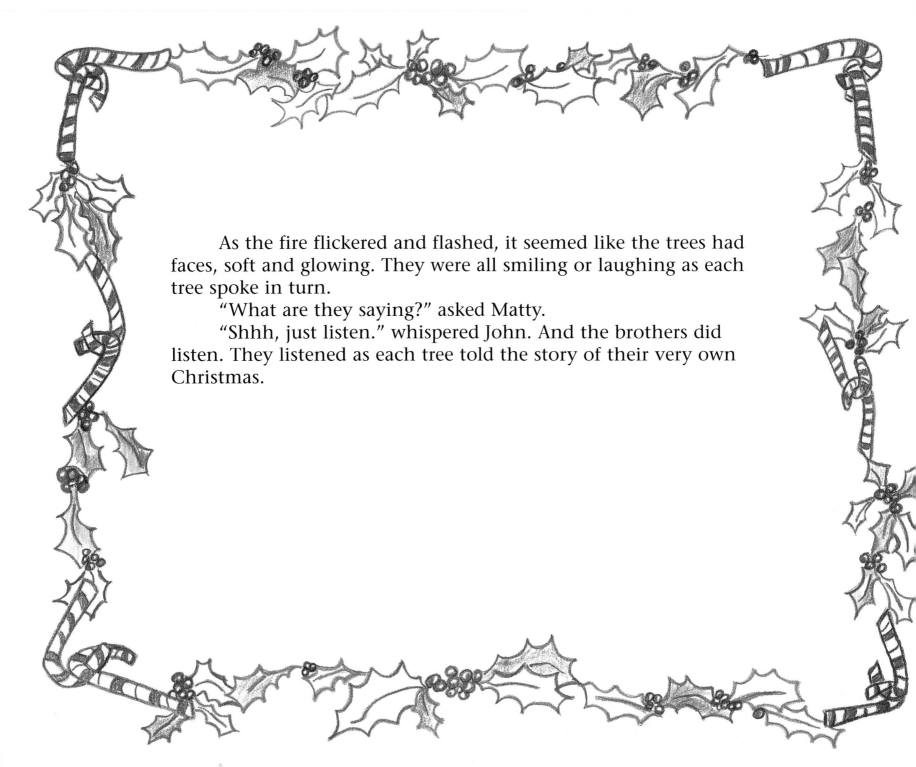

As the fire flickered and flashed, it seemed like the trees had faces, soft and glowing. They were all smiling or laughing as each tree spoke in turn.

"What are they saying?" asked Matty.

"Shhh, just listen." whispered John. And the brothers did listen. They listened as each tree told the story of their very own Christmas.

"It was a wonderful day!" said the tree with the left over tinsel. "My family had four children in it! There was so much wrapping paper I couldn't see my bottom branches! Then, to top it off their dog almost knocked me over right in the middle of it all!" The other trees started to laugh so hard that their branches swished and shook. It looked as if a strong wind was blowing.

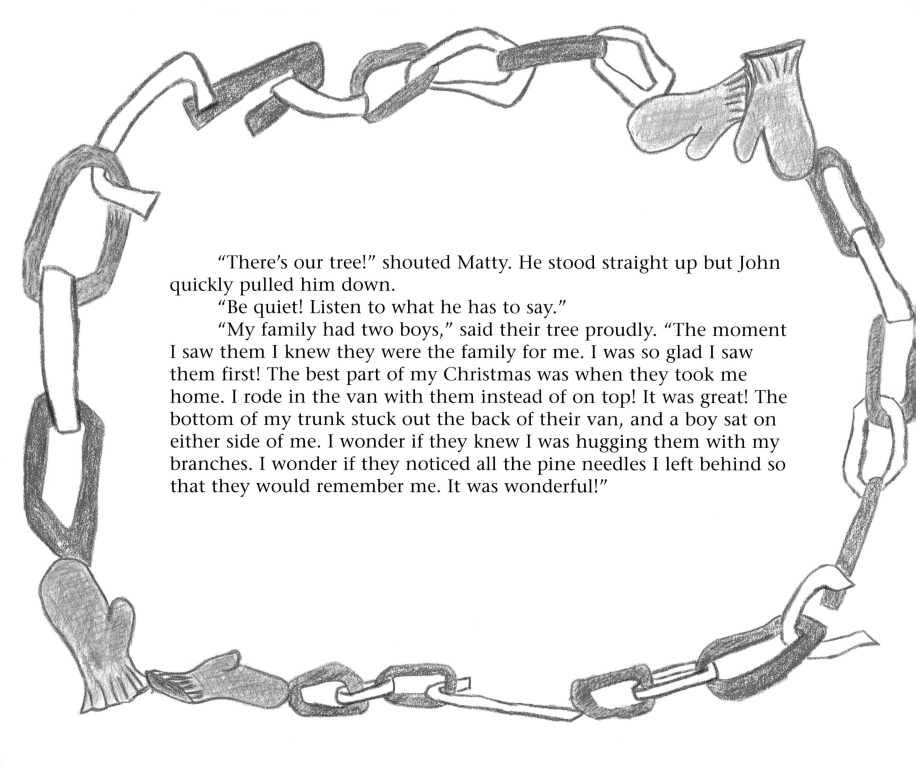

"There's our tree!" shouted Matty. He stood straight up but John quickly pulled him down.

"Be quiet! Listen to what he has to say."

"My family had two boys," said their tree proudly. "The moment I saw them I knew they were the family for me. I was so glad I saw them first! The best part of my Christmas was when they took me home. I rode in the van with them instead of on top! It was great! The bottom of my trunk stuck out the back of their van, and a boy sat on either side of me. I wonder if they knew I was hugging them with my branches. I wonder if they noticed all the pine needles I left behind so that they would remember me. It was wonderful!"

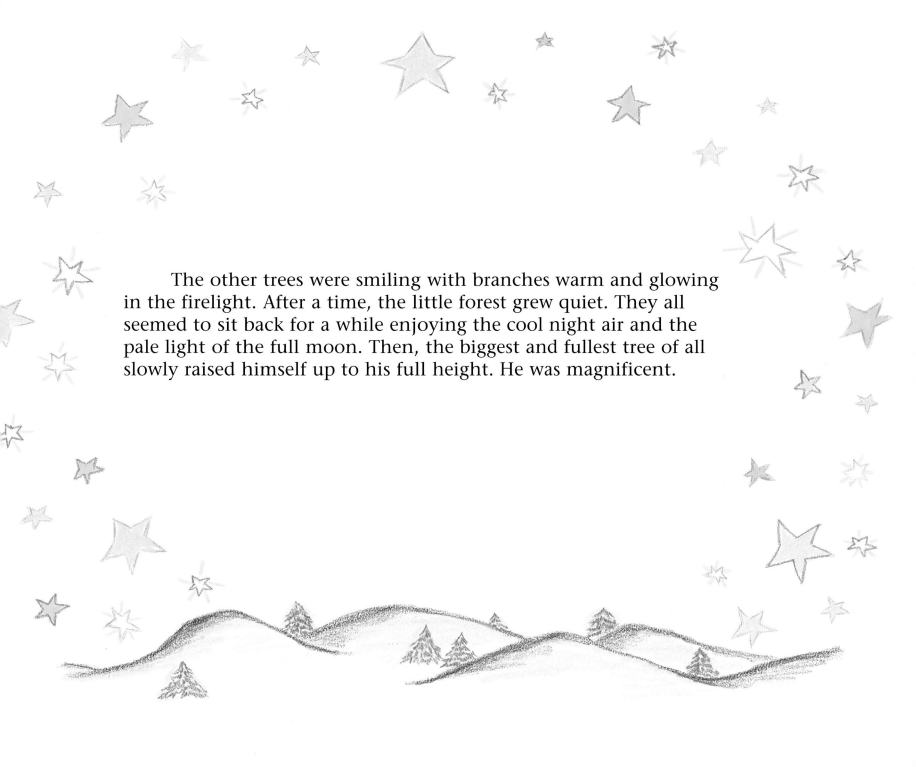

The other trees were smiling with branches warm and glowing in the firelight. After a time, the little forest grew quiet. They all seemed to sit back for a while enjoying the cool night air and the pale light of the full moon. Then, the biggest and fullest tree of all slowly raised himself up to his full height. He was magnificent.

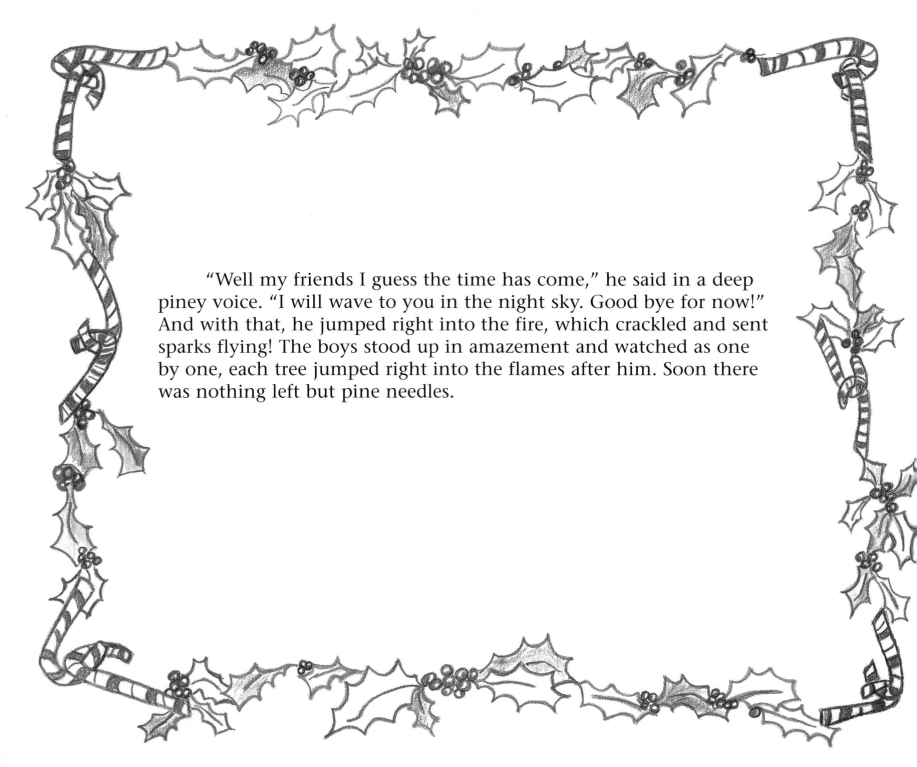

"Well my friends I guess the time has come," he said in a deep piney voice. "I will wave to you in the night sky. Good bye for now!" And with that, he jumped right into the fire, which crackled and sent sparks flying! The boys stood up in amazement and watched as one by one, each tree jumped right into the flames after him. Soon there was nothing left but pine needles.

As the brothers watched, it seemed they saw a large spark, shoot up into the night as each tree threw itself into the fire. Soon the sky was filled with the most beautiful stars the boys had ever seen. They glowed there like tiny suns until John and Matty were safely home.

J. Leopold Ferrante

That night, when the boys went to bed they watched the stars from their bedroom window.

"Look at them twinkle," said Matty. "I wonder if they are waving to each other?"

"Look," shouted John. "A shooting star!"

"Oh....and another!" said Matty. "Wow!"

"That's what happens," said John, as if he were in a dream. "That's what happens. I know what happens to the Christmas trees."

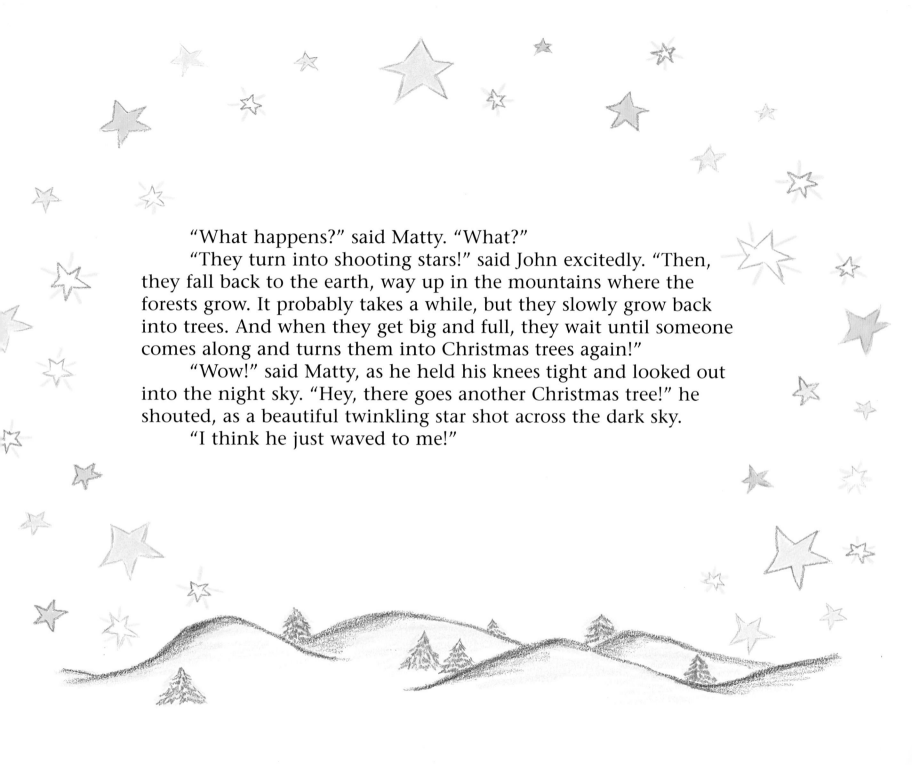

"What happens?" said Matty. "What?"

"They turn into shooting stars!" said John excitedly. "Then, they fall back to the earth, way up in the mountains where the forests grow. It probably takes a while, but they slowly grow back into trees. And when they get big and full, they wait until someone comes along and turns them into Christmas trees again!"

"Wow!" said Matty, as he held his knees tight and looked out into the night sky. "Hey, there goes another Christmas tree!" he shouted, as a beautiful twinkling star shot across the dark sky.

"I think he just waved to me!"

Published by:
Window Seat Publishing, Inc.
82 Marlborough Rd., Suite 108
West Hempstead, NY 11552

ISBN: 0-9721949-0-8

LIBRARY of CONGRESS CONTROL NUMBER: 2002108117

Printed in Hong Kong

Book Design: Budget Book Design
Printed by: BooksJustBooks.com

This is a

Window Seat Publishing

book.